Chirp!

Mary Murphy

To Aileen, Doire and Nathan – M.M.

First published 2022 by Walker Books Ltd
87 Vauxhall Walk, London SE11 5HJ

10 9 8 7 6 5 4 3 2 1

ISBN 978-1-4063-9174-9

www.walker.co.uk

Chirp!

Mary Murphy

WALKER BOOKS
AND SUBSIDIARIES
LONDON · BOSTON · SYDNEY · AUCKLAND

It has been a quiet night.
In the river,
the Heron watches
the last star fade.

Then...

Chirp,
says the Sparrow.

Warble, goes the Thrush.

Tooraloo, whistles the Blackbird from the blackberry bush.

Chee chee,
says the Wren.

Ta-tee-tee,
sings the Lark.

Tink-tink, calls the Finch.
Goodbye to
the dark.

Now the Robin pipes out with her clear, clean tune.

Ta la la,
sings the Swallow.
There goes the moon.

The Wagtails bounce and twitter,
the Starling goes *tic-tac.*

The Magpies stamp and march
and shout *chack chack chack!*

HONK, says the Goose.
Quack, goes the Duck.

The Hen in the hen house
fusses **cluck-cluck-cluck**.

The Pigeon in the apple tree says
GOO, GOO, GOO.

Then up jumps the Rooster, shouting ...

COCK-A-
DOODLE
-DOO!

tic-tac
tink-tink
chee
Tic-tac
tink-tink
chee
tink tink
chee
tic-tac
tic-tac
chirp chirp chirp
toora looo ra loO
tink-tink
chee chee
Tic-tac
tic-tac
chee
ta-tee
ta-tee
ta-tee
ta-tee
HONK
HONK tic-tac
HONK
cock-a-
chee chee chee chee
ta-tee ta-tee ta-tee
chee chee
tooraloo raloOOOO
ta-tee
ta-tee
chee chee
chee chee
cheeche chee
chee
ta-tee ta-tee
chee chee
chirp chirp chirp
quack
chee
chee chee
tink-tink
cluck cluck
chee
DOODle- tic-tac
DOO
tic-tac
chee chee
chee
chee
warble warble warble
chee chee
quack
chee chee
quack
tic-tac
tink-tink tink-tink
quack
tink-tink
quack
tink- chirp chirp chirp
tink
chack
quack quack
quack
quack

"Hush!

It's my turn to sing."

Zi...

Z

p...

Zippy...zi...

Zippy-zip...

zippy-zippy-zipp

Zippy-zippy-zippee
Zippy-zippy-zipp

Tink-tink, coo coo,
chirp chirp, tooraloo.
Honk honk, chee chee,

zippy - zippy

zippy zee!

We all have a song!
We all have something to say.

We all get to shout out for

a brand new

day!

zippeeeeee

eeezippeeeeeeeeeeeeeeeeeeeeeee

eezippzip

eeeziezip

eezippeee

eeeziezip

eezipzip zipeeeeee

eezippeeeeeeeeeeeezipzip zipeeeee

eeeeezip

ppeeeee

zippeeee

eeeeeezip

zipzipeeezippeeee